9/03 Surgeon 14.

Look Down Low

Written by Dana Meachen Rau
Illustrated by Bernard Adnet

Reading Advisers:

Gail Saunders-Smith, Ph.D., Reading Specialist

*Dr. Linda D. Labbo, Department of Reading Education,
College of Education, The University of Georgia*

LEVEL A

A COMPASS POINT

EARLY READER

For Jen

A Note to Parents

As you share this book with your child, you are showing your new reader what reading looks like and sounds like. You can read to your child any-where—in a special area in your home, at the library, on the bus, or in the car. Your child will associate reading with the pleasure of being with you.

This book will introduce your young reader to many of the basic con-cepts, skills, and vocabulary necessary for successful reading. Talk through the details in each picture before you read. Then read the book to your child. As you read, point to each word, stopping to talk about what the words mean and the pictures show. Your child will begin to link the sounds of the letters with the look of the words that you and he or she read.

After your child is familiar with the story, let him or her read the story alone. Be careful to let the young reader make mistakes and correct them on his or her own. Be sure to praise the young reader's abilities. And, above all, have fun.

Gail Saunders-Smith, Ph.D.
Reading Specialist

Consulting editor: Rebecca McEwen

Compass Point Books
3722 West 50th Street, #115
Minneapolis, MN 55410

Visit Compass Point Books on the Internet at *www.compasspointbooks.com* or e-mail your request to *custserv@compasspointbooks.com*

Library of Congress Cataloging-in-Publication Data
Rau, Dana Meachen.
    Look down low / written by Dana Meachen Rau ; illustrated by Bernard Adnet.
        p. cm. — (Compass Point early reader)
    "Level A."
    Summary: Look down low and crawl around, to see things hiding on the ground.
    ISBN 0-7565-0173-3 (hardcover)
    [1. Stories in rhyme.] I. Adnet, Bernard, ill. II. Title. III. Series.
PZ8.3.R232 Lo 2002
[E]—dc21   2001004723

Down on the ground
things crawl around.

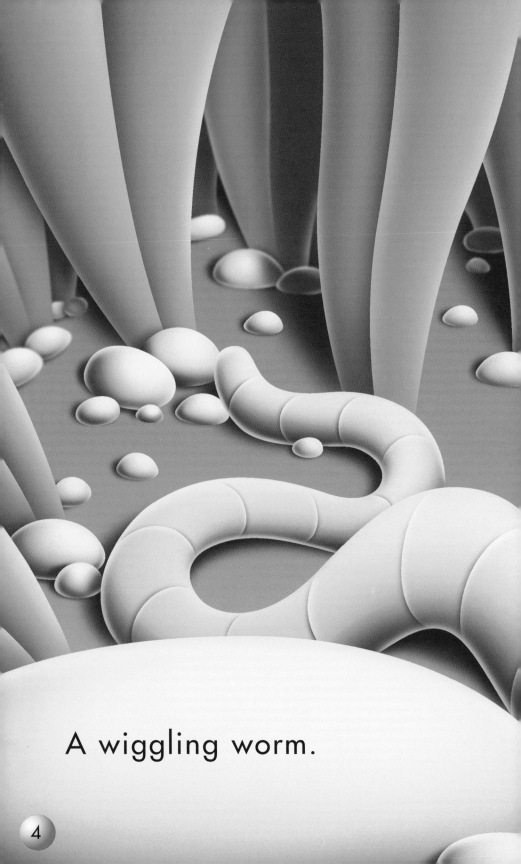

A wiggling worm.

A digging mole.

A mouse hiding in a hole.

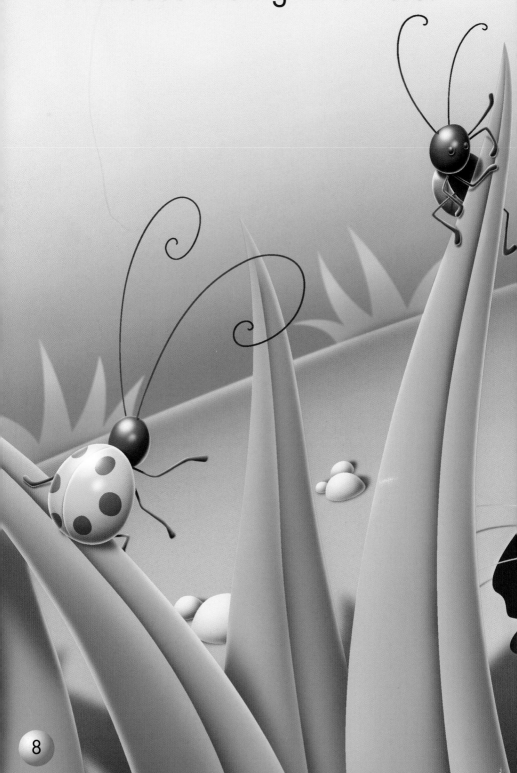

The grass is green.

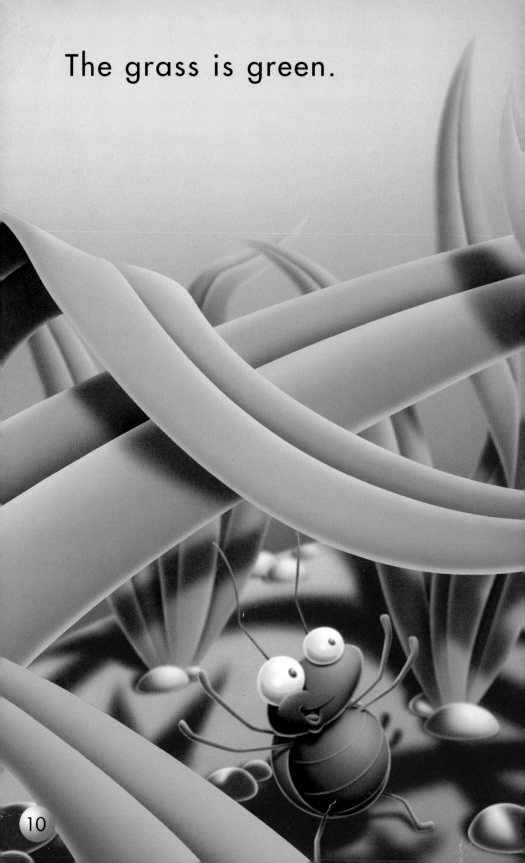

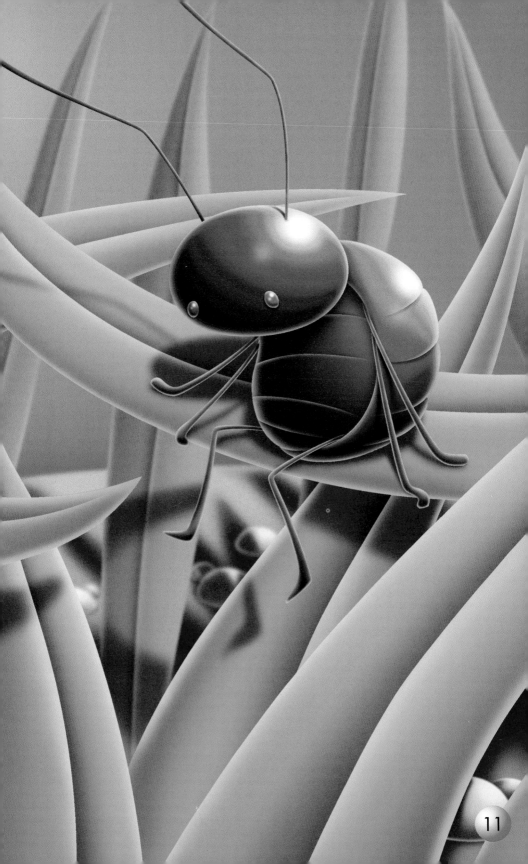

The mud is brown.

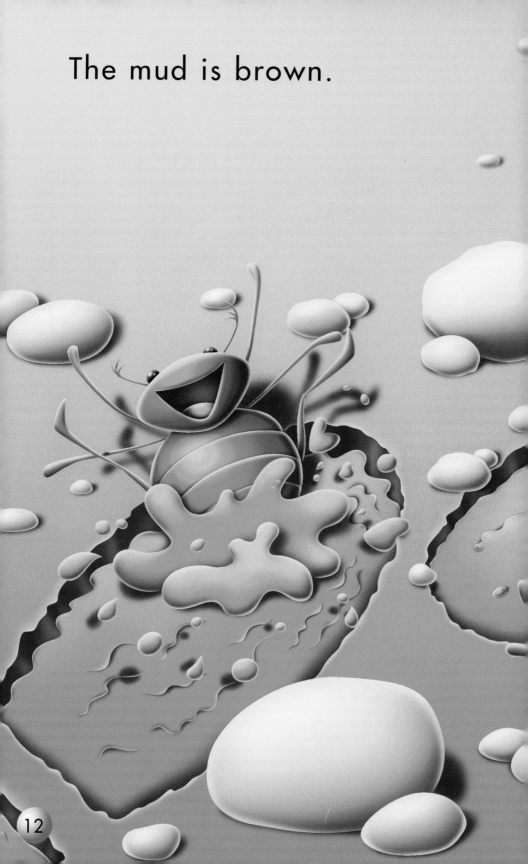

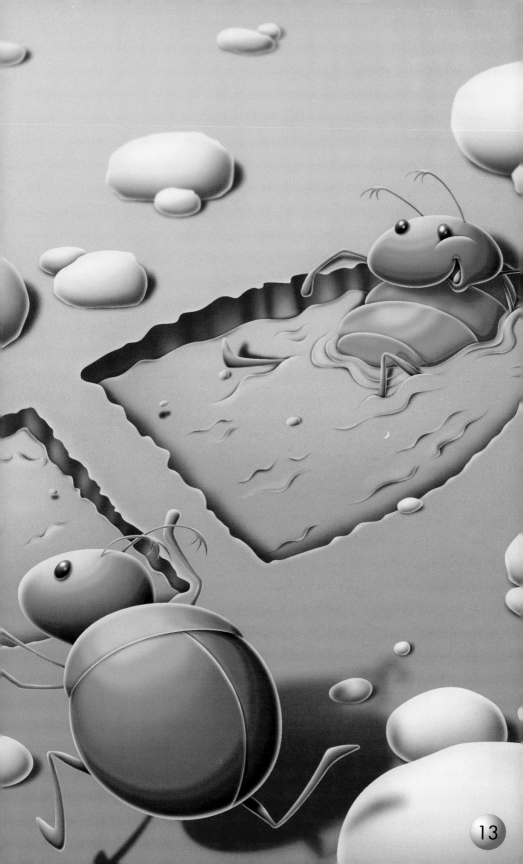

How do I see
things on the ground?

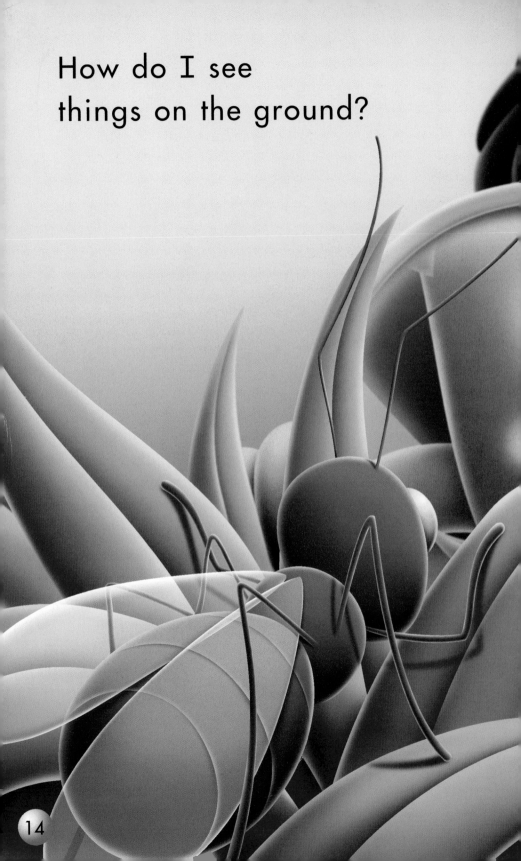

An orange flower
with a tall stem.

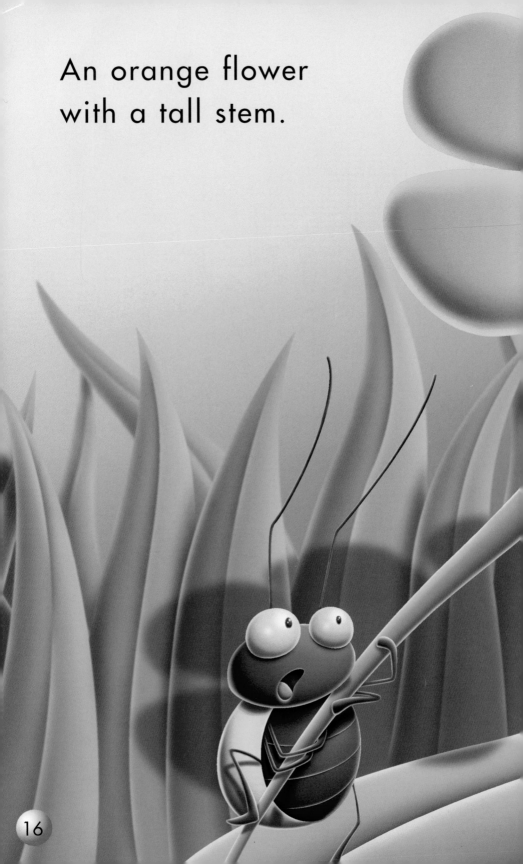

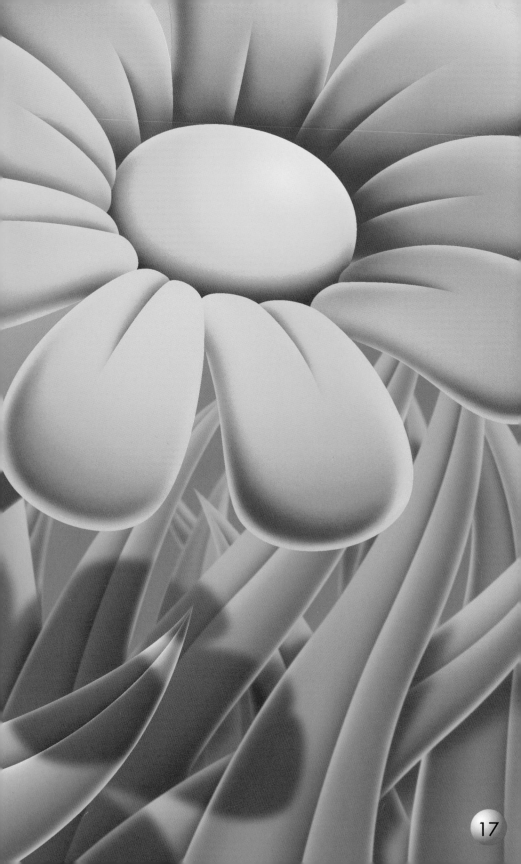

A line of ants.
There are lots of them!

How do I see
things on the ground?

I get down low
and look around!

Word List

(In this book: 42 words)

a	green	mud
an	ground	of
and	hiding	on
ants	hole	orange
are	how	see
around	I	stem
brown	in	tall
crawl	is	the
digging	line	them
do	look	there
down	lots	things
flower	low	wiggling
get	mole	with
grass	mouse	worm

About the Author
Besides writing and drawing pictures, one of Dana Rau's hobbies is gardening in her yard in Farmington, Connecticut, with her husband, Chris, and kids, Charlie and Allison. Gardening gives her a chance to dig in the dirt and see all the things buried there. She finds sticks, rocks, and worms. Someday, she hopes to find long-lost treasure.

About the Illustrator
Bernard Adnet grew up in the French Alps near the city of Grenoble. He always loved to draw, especially for his eight young nieces and nephews. After studying traditional fine arts in Paris, Bernard moved to New York City He has worked as a freelance illustrator there since 1992 His work is created using a very special blend of software programs.